THIS BLOOMSBURY BOOK

BELONGS TO

....

For Bill and Phyllis Baggaley and Uncle Martin

This edition published for Igloo Books Ltd in 2007

First published in Great Britain in 2004 by Bloomsbury Publishing Plc
38 Soho Square, London, W1D 3HB

Text and illustrations copyright © Stephen Waterhouse 2004
The moral right of the author/illustrator has been asserted

A CIP catalogue record of this book is available from the British Library

ISBN 0 7475 6474 4

Printed and bound by South China Printing Co

3 5 7 9 10 8 6 4 2

All papers used by Bloomsbury Publishing are natural, recyclable products made from wood grown in well-managed forests.
The manufacturing processes conform to the environmental regulations of the country of origin.

GET BUSY THIS SUMMER!

Stephen Waterhouse

The penguins love going on their summer holiday and cannot wait to get busy having lots of fun in the sun!

Each year they pack up all their favourite toys and clothes ...

Then they set off! Their car can go anywhere ...

...they travel high and low.

After a long journey, they finally arrive. The penguins unpack their car and set up the tent.

Soon they fall fast asleep under the twinkling stars.

There are lots of fun things for the penguins to do on holiday.

They go sailing on a great big boat ...

with Captain Polar Bear!

They pick colourful fruit in the midday heat ...

They relax in the warm afternoon sun ...

They swim and splash in the big blue sea ...

Then they go fishing ...

... and cook the tasty fish on a HOT barbecue!

They play beach games with their favourite toys ...

Then, at the end of the holiday, they pack
up all their things and set off home ...

... to cool off!

What a happy holiday!